STINKBOMB and Ketchup-Face

AND THE
BADNESS
OF BADGERS

STINKBOMB
and
Ketchup-Face

AND THE
BADNESS
OF BADGERS

ILLUSTRATED BY SAM RICKS

G. P. PUTNAM'S SONS

G. P. PUTNAM'S SONS

an imprint of Penguin Random House LLC
375 Hudson Street
New York, NY 10014

Text copyright © 2014 by John Dougherty.
Illustrations copyright © 2017 by Sam Ricks.
First published in Great Britain by Oxford University Press.
First American edition published in 2017 by G. P. Putnam's Sons.

Library of Congress Cataloging-in-Publication Data
Names: Dougherty, John, author. I Ricks, Sam, illustrator.
Title: Stinkbomb & Ketchup-Face and the badness of badgers / John Dougherty ; illustrated by Sam Ricks.
Other titles: Stinkbomb and Ketchup-Face and the badness of badgers
Description: First American edition. I New York : G. P. Putnam's Sons, 2017.
"First published in Great Britain by Oxford University Press."
Summary: Stinkbomb and his sister, Ketchup-Face, with help from King Toothbrush Weasel, go on an adventure to recover the stolen contents of their piggy bank from a gang of rascally badgers.
Identifiers: LCCN 2016000640 I ISBN 9781101996621 (hardcover)
Subjects: I CYAC: Brothers and sisters—Fiction. I Adventure and adventurers—Fiction. I Kings, queens, rulers, etc.—Fiction. I Badgers—Fiction. I Humorous stories.
Classification: LCC PZ7.D74433 St 2017 I DDC [Fic]—dc23
LC record available at https://lccn.loc.gov/2016000640
Printed in the United States of America.   ISBN 9781101996621
10 9 8 7 6 5 4 3 2 1

Design by Annie Ericsson. Text set in Warnock Pro.

For my favorite antipodean piglets,
Genevieve & Holly,
with love from your uncle John.

And—as always—for the original
Stinkbomb & Ketchup-Face,
Noah & Cara, with all my love.
More than ever, this one's for you.
—J.D.

To Seara and Elijah—partners in
crime, and Great Kerfufflers.
—S.R.

CHAPTER 1

— · —

IN WHICH
OUR HEROES WAKE UP
AND A STARTLING DISCOVERY
IS MADE

It was early morning, and dawn was breaking over the peaceful little island of Great Kerfuffle.

The golden sun peeped over the horizon, checked to make sure no one was looking, and slowly climbed into the blue sky. And far below, in a tall tree in the garden of a lovely house high on a hillside above the tiny village of Loose Pebbles, a blackbird cleared its throat and broke forth into song to greet the new day.

Inside the lovely house, in a beautiful pink bedroom, a little girl opened her eyes and leapt out of bed. Dashing to the window, she flung the shutters wide open. The sunlight streamed in, bringing with it the sweet smell of blossoms on the morning breeze. As if in greeting, the tree waved gently and rustled its leaves. There, on the nearest branch, so close she could almost touch it, perched the blackbird, trilling merrily.

"Hey! Blackbird! Shut your beak!"

yelled the little girl, and she threw a shoe at it.

The shoe bounced off the branch and fell to the ground, where it was picked up by a passing cat. The blackbird stuck out its tongue and blew a **defiant raspberry**. Then it flew away.

The little girl stomped grumpily back to her bed and shut her eyes. But it was no good: she couldn't get back to sleep. After a few minutes, she tried actually getting into the bed and lying down, but that didn't help either. So then she decided to go and jump on her brother's face.

Seconds later, in the bedroom just across the landing, the little girl's brother pulled one of her toes out of his right nostril and groaned wearily.

"Morning, Stinkbomb!" said the little girl, cheerfully **flumping** on his tummy. "Time to get up!"

"Why?" said Stinkbomb grouchily.

"Because," said the little girl, "it's a beautiful morning, and the sun is shining, and we can play games and have adventures, and if you don't get up, I'm going to put oatmeal down your pants forever, so there."

Stinkbomb thought about this. The idea of having oatmeal put down his pants forever certainly sounded interesting, but he wasn't sure he would actually like it. So he decided to get up.

As he did, he made a disturbing discovery. On his bedroom floor lay a small ceramic pig with its feet in the air and a hole in its tummy.

"Hey! Ketchup-Face!" he said grumpily. "Have you been raiding my piggy bank?"

Ketchup-Face shook her head. "Nope," she said.

"Well, *somebody* has!" said Stinkbomb. "Look!" He picked up the piggy bank and shook it. A solitary penny fell out and landed with a little *thunk* on the carpet. "I had a **twenty-dollar bill** in there, and it's gone!"

Ketchup-Face shrugged. "Wasn't me."

Stinkbomb scratched his head. His sister had many faults, but telling lies wasn't one of them.

"Well, then," he said, "it must have been the **badgers.**"

Ketchup-Face thought about this. She wasn't really sure what badgers were, so she just nodded and tried to look wise. Then she changed her mind and asked, "What's a badger?"

"It's a, it's a, well, *you* know," said Stinkbomb. "They dig holes in the lawn and eat all the worms, and they knock over garbage cans and frighten chickens and drive too fast."

"Oh," said Ketchup-Face. "And do they empty piggy banks as well?"

"Probably," Stinkbomb said knowledgeably. "It sounds like the kind of thing they *would* do."

Ketchup-Face scratched her head. It was quite a pretty head, except when the front of it was covered with  **Ketchup**

and

chocolate

and **Jam**

and **Mud.**

Just at the moment it was clean, but it was a fair bet that by the end of Chapter Four it would be filthy again.

"Does it?" she asked.

Stinkbomb nodded in a big-brotherly kind of way. "Of course it does," he said. "Think about it. They do **bad** things because they're **bad**gers. If they weren't **bad**, they'd just be **gers**. I bet our garbage can's been knocked over too."

Ketchup-Face opened the window and looked

outside. Sure enough, the family garbage can was lying on its side in the yard, giving every indication of having been badgered.

"Gosh," Ketchup-Face said, impressed, "I suppose that proves it. The badgers have taken your twenty-dollar bill. What are we going to do about it?"

Stinkbomb drew himself upright. Then he drew himself sitting down, and then he drew himself winning a race and getting a medal, and then he drew a dinosaur taking a bath. And then he put his pencil down and said, "I'll tell you what we're going to do. We're going to see the king."

CHAPTER 2

— • —

IN WHICH
OUR HEROES SET OFF TO SEE THE KING
AND KETCHUP-FACE SINGS A SONG

In most stories, if the heroes were to set off to see the king, you'd expect their journey to take a really long time. Chapters and **chapters** and **chapters**, probably, in which they'd have adventures and fight dragons and giant spiders. They'd get lost in the forest, and nearly get eaten by witches, and have to solve mysterious riddles before they could cross rivers or ravines, and all that kind of stuff. And it'd probably rain as well, and they wouldn't have brought their coats or sandwiches or anything.

Fortunately for Stinkbomb and Ketchup-Face, the nearest king lived only half a mile away. It was just five minutes on the number 47 bus if you had fifty cents each. But Stinkbomb and Ketchup-Face didn't have any money, so they set off through the fields.

It was a truly beautiful day. The sun beamed down on them like a kindly uncle, the trees waved like friendly flags, and all around them the birds twittered and tweeted like a tiny feathered choir.

All of nature was at play: they saw newts playing leap frog and frogs playing leap newt; bunnies playing leap squirrel and squirrels playing leap bunny; foxes playing leap pig and pigs playing squash fox, because pigs aren't very good at leaping and they're quite BIG.

They saw a snake basking in the sunshine, lambs frolicking in the pasture, and a shy deer in a false mustache peeping through the bushes. It was all so lovely that it made Ketchup-Face want to sing, and—since making up songs was one of her favorite things to do—that's exactly what she did.

This is what she sang:

"Blueberry Jam
Blueberry Jam
Blueberry Jam, blueberry Jam
Blueberry, blueberry, blueberry Jam
Bluey, bluey, bluey, bluey
Bluey, bluey, blueberry Jam
Blueberry Jam
Blueberry Jam
Blueberry
Jaaaaaaaaam!!!!!"

"That's a song about blueberry jam," she added.

"Very nice," said Stinkbomb. "What's it called?"

Ketchup-Face thought about this. "Ummm . . . 'Blueberry Jam,'" she said. " 'Cause it's about blueberry jam."

Stinkbomb nodded wisely. "I see," he said. He paused—tactfully, because he liked to encourage his little sister when she wasn't jumping on his face and sticking her toes up his nose—but he felt there was something about the song that left room for improvement. "Do you think it might be a bit . . . same-y?" he said eventually.

Ketchup-Face **scratched** her head. "I see what you mean," she said. "Maybe I should put some other kinds of jam in it as well."

So on they went, with Ketchup-Face trying out different kinds of jam in her song and Stinkbomb sticking his fingers in his ears, until at last they caught sight of the palace.

Ketchup-Face stopped singing and pointed. "There it is," she said happily.

"What did you say?" said Stinkbomb.

"THERE it is," repeated Ketchup-Face. **"What did you say???"** said Stinkbomb.

"I SAID, there it is!" yelled Ketchup-Face.

"What did you say???" shouted Stinkbomb.

Ketchup-Face tugged at Stinkbomb's elbows until his fingers popped out of his ears. "I said, there it is," she explained.

"Oh," said Stinkbomb. "Why didn't you say so? And by the way," he added, "why are you **hopping**?"

Ketchup-Face looked down at her feet. "Because I threw one of my shoes at a blackbird," she said. "Come on!"

And off she **hippity-hopped** again, with Stinkbomb *strolling* along behind her, until they reached the palace.

CHAPTER 3

—•—

IN WHICH WE LEARN A LITTLE HISTORY

Not many children live only half a mile from a real king, but then not many children live near the tiny village of **Loose Pebbles** on the little island of **Great Kerfuffle**. **Loose Pebbles** is the capital village of **Great Kerfuffle**, which is too small to have a capital city or even a capital town; even so, **Great Kerfuffle** is very rare among little islands, because it has its very own king all to itself.

The reason for this dates back to the English **Wars of the Roses**. There was an argument between **King Richard III** and **King Henry VII** as to which of them was really the king, and they agreed that the best way to find out who was right was to put lots of men in a field and get them to hit each other with pointy things. What most people don't know is that there was a third man who thought he was king. He was known as **King Isabel the Confused**, and he kept showing up at battles and trying to join in. The problem was that **King Isabel** hadn't really gotten the hang of battling, and he and his soldiers just ended up getting in the way and shouting things like:

"Put that pointy thing down!"

"You'll poke someone's eye out if you're not careful!"

The effect was something like when a small dog tries to take part in a soccer game. The dog has no chance of winning, but it makes it very difficult for anyone else to either. So in the end, **King Richard** and **King Henry** decided that the only way to get on with the battle was to give **King Isabel** a little kingdom of his very own, as long as he promised to go away and stop being a pain.

The kingdom they gave him was, of course, **Great Kerfuffle**, which at that time was at the very tip of southwestern England. As soon as **King Isabel** had been crowned as its king, **King Henry** tiptoed down in the dead of night, sawed it off, and sent it floating out to sea. **King Richard** would have helped, but he couldn't on account of having lost the battle and so being extremely dead.

And that is why **Great Kerfuffle** has its very own king.

The king on the throne now was a great-great-great-great-great-great-great-great-great-great-great-great-great- on and on forever lots and lots of times great-great-great- this is getting a bit boring great-great-great-great-great-great-great- grandson of **King Isabel the Confused**, and his name was **King Sandra**—or, at least, it had been until recently. However, he had worried that perhaps **King Sandra** was a silly name, and had decided to change it to something more sensible.

Unfortunately, he had made the mistake of asking the citizens of **Great Kerfuffle** to choose his new, sensible name, which is why he was now known as **King Toothbrush Weasel.**

"REX PENICULUS DENTIUM MUSTELA"

King Toothbrush Weasel lived, of course, in a palace—the very palace that Stinkbomb and Ketchup-Face had just reached.

You remember. At the end of Chapter Two. And now it's the end of Chapter Three.

CHAPTER 4

IN WHICH OUR HEROES MEET THE ARMY

King Toothbrush Weasel's palace wasn't very big. In fact, it was about the size of a small cottage. It had pretty little towers with thatched turrets, and dinky little battlements, and the sweetest little sentry box you've ever seen, and in the little sentry box the entire army of **Great Kerfuffle** was standing guard.

You might think that it would be a bit of a **squeeze**, fitting an entire army into one little sentry box. But you'd be wrong. Great Kerfuffle was, of course, a very small kingdom, and it couldn't afford a big army with lots of soldiers. In fact, there was only one soldier in the army of Great Kerfuffle, and he was a cat named Malcolm the Cat.

Stinkbomb and Ketchup-Face looked down at him. He was a small gray cat with one shoe and a little red soldier's jacket. He also had one of those tall, furry black hats, just like the guards outside Buckingham Palace wear, but he never wore it because it would have covered him completely and left him unable to move. Instead, he was lying on it, to make himself look **taller** without actually having to stand up.

"And what do *you* want?" said Malcolm the Cat, in a tone of voice that suggested he wasn't really interested unless it involved a can opener and a can of cat food.

"We'd like to see King Toothbrush Weasel, please," said Ketchup-Face.

"Why?" asked Malcolm the Cat.

"Because the badgers have stolen my money," Stinkbomb said.

Malcolm the Cat sat up and stared at them both without blinking, until they felt a bit uncomfortable. "All right, then," he said eventually. "You can knock on the door."

Then, as Stinkbomb raised his hand to knock, the cat said, "Actually, you can't."

Stinkbomb dropped his hand. "Why not?" he said.

Malcolm the Cat looked at him, as if thinking. "No, I suppose you can," he said.

Stinkbomb's hand went to the knocker.

"STOP!" said Malcolm the Cat.

Stinkbomb stopped and looked at him.

"Oh, go on, then," said Malcolm the Cat. As Stinkbomb raised his hand again, he added, "Sorry, you can't after all. My mistake."

"But . . ." began Stinkbomb.

"Oh, all right," Malcolm the Cat said. After a pause, during which Stinkbomb looked at him suspiciously, he said, "No, go on. Really. You can knock on the door. You have my official permission."

"Really?" said Stinkbomb.

"Really," said Malcolm the Cat. "Honest. Go on."

Stinkbomb raised his hand to the knocker.

"Oh, wait," said Malcolm the Cat. "Sorry. You can't knock on the door after all."

Ketchup-Face gave Malcolm the Cat the special glare she reserved for especially annoying people and parents who wouldn't give her chocolate. "What are you doing?" she asked.

"Sorry," said Malcolm the Cat. "Just playing with you. Force of habit. I won't do it again. You can knock on the door now. Oh, whoops," he added as Stinkbomb went once more to knock, "my mistake. You can't."

It could have gone on like this for some time, if Stinkbomb hadn't remembered that he had a fish in his pocket. Stinkbomb was the kind of boy whose pockets were always full of things that might come in handy later, and it occurred to him that if you are dealing with an uncooperative cat, the best way to win it over is with a nice fat fish.

So he pulled the fish out of his pocket, and with a mighty **WHAM!** he knocked Malcolm the Cat off the furry hat with it. Before Malcolm the Cat could pick himself up again, Stinkbomb had knocked on the palace door.

CHAPTER 5

—— • ——

IN WHICH OUR HEROES MEET THE KING

Immediately they heard from inside the palace the sound of footsteps, quiet at first but **getting louder**. They waited, both of them feeling the warm sun on their backs and the soft breeze in their hair, and Stinkbomb feeling a gentle tugging at his side, which turned out to be Malcolm the Cat trying to climb into his pocket to get the fish.

Eventually, the door opened, and there stood King Toothbrush Weasel, wearing a yellow-checked bathrobe on which was pinned a little badge that said  Butler .

"Yes?" said King Toothbrush Weasel.

"Hello, King Toothbrush Weasel," said Ketchup-Face, grinning her special grin that she kept for important people. She was particularly proud of this grin at the moment, as it showed the gap where she had recently lost a tooth.

King Toothbrush Weasel gave Ketchup-Face a stern look. "I am not King Toothbrush Weasel," he said firmly, tapping the little badge that said **Butler**. "I am the butler. Now, what do you want?"

"We've come to see King Toothbrush Weasel," said Stinkbomb.

"And who shall I say is calling?" asked King Toothbrush Weasel.

"Ketchup-Face and Stinkbomb," said Ketchup-Face, who was tired of always being second.

"Stinkbomb and Ketchup-Face," corrected Stinkbomb, who liked to insist on his own rights as the older sibling.

"Ketchup-Face and Stinkbomb and Stinkbomb and Ketchup-Face," repeated King Toothbrush Weasel. "Come in. Oh," he added, "and do get out of the boy's pocket, Malcolm the Cat. You're supposed to be on guard duty."

They entered the palace and found themselves in a small and cluttered entrance hall. King Toothbrush Weasel **squeezed** past a bicycle that was leaning against the radiator, said, "Please follow me," and began walking in place, at first thumping his feet on the floor as **loudly** as he could, but getting **gradually** quieter.

Stinkbomb and Ketchup-Face looked at each other, puzzled. King Toothbrush Weasel glanced over his shoulder at them and halted.

"Do come along," he said.

"But you're not going anywhere," Ketchup-Face pointed out. "You're just walking in place and making your footsteps **quieter**."

King Toothbrush Weasel turned indignantly. "I am not walking in place," he said. "I am walking down a very long corridor in a large and impressive palace! And my footsteps are getting quieter because I am getting farther away. Now come along!"

Stinkbomb and Ketchup-Face shrugged and began to walk in place. Satisfied, King Toothbrush Weasel turned again and led the way without actually going anywhere.

Before very long, they reached a door that they'd been standing beside the whole time.

"Please wait here," King Toothbrush Weasel said, "and I shall ask if His Majesty will see you."

He stepped through the door, and Stinkbomb and Ketchup-Face heard him say: "Ketchup-Face and Stinkbomb and Stinkbomb and Ketchup-Face to see you, Your Majesty."

And then they heard him say, "Oh, dear. It's so very, very busy being a king, you know. I was just about to do some busy kingly things, and look at some royal bits of paper, and stuff like that. But I suppose the needs of my subjects must come first. Do show them in."

And then they heard him say, "Very good, Your Majesty."

He popped his head out and said, "King Toothbrush Weasel will see you now."

Stinkbomb and Ketchup-Face went in and waited politely while King Toothbrush Weasel took off the badge that said **Butler** , put on a small crown and a badge that said King , and sat down on a comfy armchair that was

trimmed with tinsel and had a label on it saying
 .

"Welcome, loyal subjects," he said. Then he added worriedly, "You are loyal subjects, I suppose? I wouldn't like to think you were the disloyal sort. Are you loyal subjects?"

"Oh, yes," said Stinkbomb.

"What's '**LoyaL SubJectS**'?" asked Ketchup-Face. "**Ow**," she added as Stinkbomb elbowed her in the ribs. "What'd you do that for? I only asked because he said, and anyway, **OW**," she went on as Stinkbomb elbowed her again. "Oh, all right, yes we are, whatever it is, as long as it doesn't involve spinach."

King Toothbrush Weasel looked relieved. "Oh, good," he said. "Now," he continued, smiling at Ketchup-Face, "you must be Ketchup-Face and Stinkbomb, and you"—he turned to Stinkbomb—"must be Stinkbomb and Ketchup-Face. You're very young to be coming to the palace all by yourselves. Haven't you brought your parents with you?"

"No, Your Majesty," said Stinkbomb.

"They like to keep out of the way when we're in a story," explained Ketchup-Face. "'Cause parents spoil stories if they're in them. They just hang around stopping you from having adventures and making sure you wash your hands before you touch anything."

"Very wise," said King Toothbrush Weasel. Then he sat up straight and looked at her. "Wait a minute," he said. "Do you mean you're in a story now? This minute?"

"Oh, yes," said Ketchup-Face. "You can tell because of all the chapters and page numbers and stuff."

"But . . . but . . . am *I* in the story too?" asked King Toothbrush Weasel worriedly.

"Yup!" said Ketchup-Face happily.

"Yes, Your Majesty," Stinkbomb agreed. "You don't mind, do you?"

"But I'm in my bathrobe!" said King Toothbrush Weasel. "I can't be in a story in my bathrobe! Just wait here a minute!"

And he jumped up and fled the room.

CHAPTER 6

— • —

IN WHICH
KING TOOTHBRUSH WEASEL
GOES UPSTAIRS TO GET DRESSED
AND COMES BACK DOWN AGAIN

Upstairs, King Toothbrush Weasel put on some nice purple underwear with golden crowns all over. Then he chose some purple pants and a white shirt and a velvet robe trimmed with pretend fur, and got dressed. He went to the dressing table, brushed his long golden beard, and put it on. Finally he combed his hair, straightened his crown, and went downstairs again.

"Right," he said as he entered. "What did you two want to see me about?"

"Well, Your Majesty," Stinkbomb said, "we

wanted to ask for your help because the badgers have stolen a twenty-dollar bill out of my piggy bank."

"**Badgers?**" said King Toothbrush Weasel. "Impossible! There are no badgers in the kingdom of Great Kerfuffle! I banned them all by royal decree!"

"Do you think the badgers know that?" asked Ketchup-Face.

"Of course they do," said King Toothbrush Weasel. "Anyway, I'd have noticed if Great Kerfuffle was full of badgers, all *galumphing* about, being too heavy, and spiking things with those big horns on the ends of their noses."

"Um, actually I think that sounds more like rhinoceroses," said Stinkbomb.

"No, no, no," said King Toothbrush Weasel. "Rhinoceroses are those little creatures that go 'squeak' and eat cheese and are frightened of the army!"

"I thought those were mouses," said Ketchup-Face.

"Nonsense!" said King Toothbrush Weasel. "I'll prove it to you!" He went to the bookshelf, took down a book called **How to Identify a Rhinoceros**, and leafed through it.

"Ah," he said after a minute. "It does appear that I might have banned rhinoceroses instead of badgers. Oh, well, never mind. I'll just have to send someone on a mission to drive all badgers from the kingdom. You'll do. Off you go."

CHAPTER 7

———— • ————

IN WHICH
OUR HEROES SET OFF
ON THEIR QUEST

A minute later, Stinkbomb and Ketchup-Face found themselves leaving the palace with no clear idea of where to go or how to get there and a firm instruction from King Tooth-brush Weasel to rid the kingdom of every badger within its borders by lunchtime.

Stinkbomb was a little annoyed by this turn of events, but Ketchup-Face was untroubled.

"Don't worry, Stinkbomb," she said cheerfully. "We've been sent on a quest by the king, so prob-ably something will happen to help us."

"Like what?" Stinkbomb grumbled. It was nearly mid-morning, and he'd only had one breakfast and no snacks, so he was a bit grumpy.

"Oh, you know," said Ketchup-Face. "We'll probably meet some animals that're in trouble and need help, and we'll help them 'cause we're kind and nice, and then they'll give us a magical thing that'll help us when we need help, and then everyone'll have been helped and it'll all be nice."

Stinkbomb rolled his eyes. "Don't be silly," he said. "That sort of thing only happens in stories."

"But we *are* in a story," Ketchup-Face pointed out.

"Oh, yeah," said Stinkbomb. "I forgot."

And just at that moment, they heard a rather bored voice saying, "Help. Oh, help. Oh, dear me, help."

"Told you," said Ketchup-Face.

They followed the sound of the voice until it led them to a small gray cat in a red soldier's jacket.

"Oh, help," said the cat, without much enthusiasm. "Help, help, help, oh help, help. Help."

"Hello, poor dear sweet little cat," said Ketchup-Face. "Whatever can be the matter?"

"Oh, help," said the cat flatly. "Help, help, help, for my tail is tangled up with this bit of grass and I cannot get free."

"Really?" said Stinkbomb. "Your tail is tangled up with a bit of grass?"

The cat just shrugged.

Quickly, Ketchup-Face got down on one knee and freed the cat—a task that, it has to be said, required no effort at all.

"There!" she said. "And now you are free, little cat!"

"Oh, hooray," said the cat, with no more emotion than before, and twitching its tail only a little. "I am free. Hurrah, hurrah, hurrah. Hurrah. Oh, how can I ever thank you."

"Well," said Ketchup-Face, "since you asked, you could give us a magical item to help us on our quest."

The cat stared at her, without blinking, in what can only be described as a sarcastic manner. "Oh, what a good idea," it said. "Why didn't I think of that." And then it stared some more.

"So . . ." said Stinkbomb after a long and awkward pause. "Is that what you're going to do?"

"I suppose so," said the cat reluctantly. "Here. Because you have saved me from this terrible and dangerous bit of grass, I shall give you . . . this shoe."

It produced a rather familiar-looking item of footwear and offered it to Ketchup-Face.

"Why, thank you, little cat," said Ketchup-Face, reaching out to take it.

Just as she was about to take it, the cat snatched it away. "Oh, sorry," it said. "Maybe that wasn't the thing I was supposed to give you after all. Let me think. Oh, yes, it was. Here you are."

It held out the shoe once again. Ketchup-Face reached for it. The cat snatched it away.

As it held out the shoe a third time, it noticed Stinkbomb's hand moving toward his pocket. Hurriedly it dropped the shoe on the grass.

"Thank you, sweet little cat," said Ketchup-Face, picking it up. "And how will this magic shoe help me?"

"Well," said the cat, "if ever you are in danger . . ."

"Yes?" said Ketchup-Face.

". . . you can put it on and run away. It's quicker than hopping," said the cat, and it turned and disappeared into the long grass with no apparent fear at all of getting its tail entangled again.

"Told you!" said Ketchup-Face happily, tying the shoe around her neck so it wouldn't get lost and then h**o**pp**i**ng on ahead once more, singing to herself. Stinkbomb followed on behind, stopping occasionally to pick up an interesting thing and put it in his pocket.

After a while, Stinkbomb said, "We don't know if we're going the right way, you know."

"Don't worry," said Ketchup-Face. "I expect the next animal we meet will be able to tell us."

And just at that moment, they heard another little voice saying, "Help!
Help!"

but this one sounded as if it really meant it.

CHAPTER 8

—— • ——

IN WHICH
OUR HEROES OFFER HELP
AND ARE HELPED IN RETURN

Help!" shouted the little voice again, and as they got closer, they could hear frantic splashing noises as well.

"This way!" said Stinkbomb, and he ran ahead, with Ketchup-Face hopping along behind him. Soon they came to a grassy bank that sloped down to a stream, and there they saw a heartbreaking sight. Struggling for dear life, upside down in the water and clearly unable to swim, was a little shopping cart, which waved its wheels helplessly in the air.

"DON'T WORRY, Little SHOPPing caRt! We'LL Save you!"

shouted Ketchup-Face as she and Stinkbomb plunged down the bank and into the raging torrent, which came all the way up to their ankles.

Together, they pulled the cart out and set it upright, placing it carefully on its wheels on the bank.

"Oh, thank you! Thank you!" gasped the shopping cart. "You have saved me! How can I ever repay you?"

"Well," said Ketchup-Face, "we're on a quest to find the badgers. I don't suppose you know where they live, do you?"

"Why, yes, I do!" said the little shopping cart happily. "They live in the next valley, by a magical stream in the middle of an enchanted wood, just next to a small apartment building. Jump into my basket and I will take you there."

Stinkbomb and Ketchup-Face scrambled into the basket, and at once the little shopping cart began to race up the grassy bank.

It was terribly exciting. Imagine going on a magical horse ride, on the most beautiful horse you have ever seen.

Now imagine that the horse has a **squeaky wheel** and a saddle made out of hard wire that makes a crisscross pattern on your bottom.

Now imagine that the horse can't go in a straight line, and keeps veering off to one side. And now imagine that the horse isn't a horse at all, but is in fact a little shopping cart.

That's what it was like.

Stinkbomb and Ketchup-Face thought it was great. Stinkbomb invented a game called **BUG-CATCHER**, which involved holding his mouth open and seeing how many bugs he could catch. He gave himself one point for a fly, two points for a beetle, four points for a wasp, and a million points for an elephant. Ketchup-Face, meanwhile, sat at the front of the basket, making horsey noises and shouting things like, **"GIDDYUP!"**

"I shall call you Starlight," she said to the shopping cart.

"Actually," said the shopping cart, "my name's Eric."

Ketchup-Face was the sort of child who never let facts get in the way of a good game. "Giddyup, Starlight!" she said, and added to Stinkbomb, "Well, we've met a cat who gave us a shoe, and a horsey who gave us a ride . . ."

"I'm not a horsey," the shopping cart pointed out.

". . . so I wonder who we'll meet next?"

"A million!" answered Stinkbomb happily, pulling something out of his mouth and examining it. "I've caught an elephant!"

"Don't worry, elephant," said Ketchup-Face. "Stinkbomb has bravely saved you from his own mouth. Now you can give us something magical to help us on our quest."

Then she looked closer. "Wait a minute," she said. "That's not an elephant. It's a beetle with a big nose."

The elephant, if that's what it was, made a little *buzzing* noise and flew away.

Sometime later, the little shopping cart drew to a halt.

"I can take you no farther," it said sadly, "for we have reached the enchanted wood where the badgers dwell."

Stinkbomb and Ketchup-Face looked, but they could see no wood before them.

"Gosh!" said Stinkbomb. "It really is enchanted, isn't it? It's invisible!"

"Er, no," said the little shopping cart. "You're just facing the wrong way."

"Oh," said Stinkbomb and Ketchup-Face together. They turned around, and there, dark and forbidding, stood the enchanted wood.

"You must carry on alone," the shopping cart continued, "for the bracken and brambles are too thick for my little wheels to get through. Besides, I promised my mom I'd clean my room this afternoon. But if you ever need help, call me and I will answer. Unless I'm busy or too far away to hear or watching a good show on TV or something. Farewell, Stinkbomb and Ketchup-Face!"

"Farewell, Starlight, my noble steed!" said Ketchup-Face, trying to fling her arms around the little shopping cart's neck, but then realizing it didn't have one and settling for patting it on the handle instead.

"Yeah, bye, shopping cart," said Stinkbomb. "Thanks for the ride."

They waved good-bye until the little shopping cart was out of sight, and then turned and began to walk into the wood.

CHAPTER 9

— · —

IN WHICH

OUR HEROES WALK INTO THE WOOD
AND HAVE A STRANGE ENCOUNTER

I t's a bit scary, isn't it?" Ketchup-Face said as they walked deeper into the wood.

Stinkbomb reached out to her. "You can hold my hand if it makes you feel better," he said. **"OOF!"** he added as he fell over. "That's not my hand, it's my foot."

"Sorry," said Ketchup-Face. "It's a bit dark and gloomy in here. Do you have a flashlight?"

"I think so," said Stinkbomb, picking himself up and rummaging in his pockets. "Yes—here's one." He pulled it out and tried to switch it on, but it turned out to be a corn dog, so he ate it. Then he tried again and eventually produced a small flashlight shaped like a squirrel in a bow tie, which played "The Wheels on the Bus" when he pushed the switch. It gave out only a very dim light, but it was better than nothing.

They set off again. The thick bracken and tangled brambles made it hard going, and the dim beam from the flashlight flickered all around, casting strange shadows.

After a while, Ketchup-Face said, "Why's the light so wobbly and shaking?"

"Because I can't hold it steady," explained Stinkbomb.

"Why not?" asked Ketchup-Face.

"Because I'm **hopping**," Stinkbomb said.

"Oh," said Ketchup-Face. "Why are you **hopping**? You've got two shoes on."

"Yes," said Stinkbomb, "but you're still holding my foot."

"Oh, okay," said Ketchup-Face. "I wonder if

we're going to meet someone else soon who can help us find the badgers."

Stinkbomb shrugged. "Another animal, you mean?" he said. "There are probably lots of animals in here."

"Yes, but actually, it might not be an animal this time," said Ketchup-Face, who considered herself something of an expert on stories. "It might be a strange little man. In lots of old stories, when the heroes are on a quest, it gets to a part where they need help, and then they meet someone who's going to help them, and it says something like, 'Just then, they met the strangest little man they had ever seen.'"

Just then, they met the strangest little man they had ever seen. He had bright, beady little eyes, and little round ears, and a pointy, triangular face, and he was covered in thick gray and black fur—except for his head, which was white with two thick black stripes running from nose to neck. His legs were short and stumpy, and he had four of them, one at each corner.

Oh, and he had a fat stubby little tail, and his breath smelled like worms and garbage cans, and he was standing in a clearing spray-painting the words **BADGERS RULE** on a tree.

"Hello, strange little man," said Ketchup-Face cheerily. "Are you going to help us on our quest?"

"Depends," said the strange little man, jumping guiltily and hiding his spray can. "What kind of quest is it?"

"Well," said Ketchup-Face,

"I am Ketchup-Face and this is Stinkbomb, and we have been sent by the king to rid the kingdom of all badgers!"

"Yes," said Stinkbomb, "but we need to find them first."

The strange little man's beady little eyes narrowed, becoming even more beady and even more little. "Is that so?" he said. "And why would you want to get rid of the badgers?"

"Because we have found out all about their **evil** and **wicked** doings," said Ketchup-Face, who had a strong sense of the dramatic.

"What?" said the strange little man, his sharp little face looking suddenly worried. "**ALL** about their evil and wicked doings?"

"Oh, yes," said Ketchup-Face. "Or, at least, all about all the evil and wicked doings we've found out about. I suppose they might have done others."

"I see," said the strange little man thoughtfully.

"So," said Stinkbomb, "can you take us to the place where the badgers live? It's by a magical stream, just next to a small apartment building."

"Um, not sure," said the strange little man thoughtfully. "But I've got lots of friends, and some of them might be able to help. Just wait here—I'll be back in a few minutes."

And, dropping his spray can, he disappeared into the undergrowth.

Stinkbomb and Ketchup-Face waited.

After a moment, Stinkbomb said, "Ketchup-Face?"

"Yes?" said Ketchup-Face.

"Do you think you could let go of my foot now?"

"Um, okay," said Ketchup-Face, and she did. After another minute or two, Ketchup-Face said, "Stinkbomb?"

"Yes?" said Stinkbomb.

"Why do chapters always have to end just when something's happening?"

"What do you mean?" asked Stinkbomb.

"Well," said Ketchup-Face, "like when we got to the palace, or when King Toothbrush Weasel went upstairs to get dressed. It's always when something's happening. They never end when you're just standing around waiting or something like that."

"They could, though," said Stinkbomb.

"Could they?"

"Yeah," said Stinkbomb knowledgeably. "Chapters can end whenever they like. They could even end in the middle of a

CHAPTER 10

IN WHICH
STINKBOMB FINISHES HIS SENTENCE
AND OUR HEROES FIND THEMSELVES
IN TERRIBLE DANGER

sentence, if they wanted to."

"Gosh!" said Ketchup-Face, impressed.

Just then, the strange little man reappeared.

"Hello again, strange little man," said Ketchup-
Face brightly.

"Er, yeah, hello," the strange little man said gruffly. "I've brought lots of other strange little men. Maybe one of them can help you."

And suddenly, the clearing was full of strange little men, all of them looking very much like the first, and most of them with rather unpleasant expressions on their pointy stripy furry faces.

"Hello, strange little men!" said Ketchup-Face.

"Right. So, all you other, um, strange little men," said the first strange little man meaningfully, "these two are here because they've found out about all the badgers' evil and wicked doings that they've been doing evilly and wickedly. So we're going to, um, help them find the badgers." There was some muttering among the strange little men, and they shuffled forward in a way that Stinkbomb and Ketchup-Face did not find entirely comfortable.

And then one of them—a particularly small strange little man with a high squeaky voice—said, in a puzzled tone: "But we are the badgers."

"Shhh! Shut up, Stewart the Badger!"

hissed all the other badgers, because that is what they were. But it was too late—Stinkbomb and Ketchup-Face had heard.

Ketchup-Face's eyes narrowed. "You never said you were badgers," she said accusingly.

"Er, we're not," said one of the badgers. "We're, er, lemmings. Isn't that right, Rolf the Badger?"

"That's right," agreed Rolf the Badger, a big badger with a big badge that said "We're not badgers at all. Are we, Harry the Badger?"

"No," agreed Harry the Badger, taking a sip of tea from a mug marked "We're not even slightly badgery. Are we, Stewart the Badger?"

"Yes, we are," said Stewart the Badger cheerfully.

Harry the Badger passed him a note that said:

Stewart the Badger read it slowly three times and then added, "Er, no, we're not."

He turned the note over. On the other side it said:

Pretend you're
a lemming.

"Er, I'm a lemming," he added.

Ketchup-Face smiled a relieved sort of smile. "Oh, well, that's all right, then," she said. "Can you tell us where to find the badgers?"

But Stinkbomb was not so easily fooled. He reached into his pocket and pulled out a book he had borrowed from King Toothbrush Weasel. It was called *The Wrong Book*, but it was the wrong book, so he put it back and pulled out another one, called *How to Identify a Badger*. He leafed through it quickly, noting the badgers' stripy heads, gray and black fur, and thick, muscular bodies. "Are you sure you're not badgers?" he asked suspiciously.

"Oh, yes," said all the badgers. "Quite sure."

Stinkbomb turned to the chapter entitled "Absolutely Foolproof Ways to Identify a Badger," read it carefully, and then reached into his pocket and pulled out a garbage can, a chicken, and a sports car.

Immediately, the badgers knocked over the garbage can,

frightened
the chicken,

and drove the
sports car
too fast.

Stinkbomb's eyes widened as he realized the danger they were in. **"It's the badgers!"** he yelled. **"RUN!"**

"Okay," said Ketchup-Face, sitting down. "Can you help me with my shoelaces? **Oof!**" she added as she disappeared under a pile of badgers.

Stinkbomb was outraged.

"That's not fair!" he said.

Rolf the Badger looked up from his position on top of the pile. "Isn't it?" he said.

"No, it's not!" said Stinkbomb firmly. "She hadn't finished putting her shoe on. It's cheating to jump on her before she's ready."

The badgers blushed. "Sorry," they mumbled, and got off Ketchup-Face. Stewart the Badger even helped her with her shoelace, just to make amends.

"Right," said Stinkbomb. "Now you have to give us a head start."

"Okay," agreed the badgers, and they closed their eyes and began to count to a hundred.

They'd gotten as far as thirty-seven when Harry the Badger opened his eyes and said, "Hang on! We're not *supposed* to be fair! We're the bad guys!"

All the other badgers took their paws away from their faces and said, "Oh, *yeah*! I forgot!"—all, that is, except Stewart the Badger, who said, "*Are* we? Awwww!"

"Get them!"

cried Rolf the Badger.

"Er . . . get who?" asked Stewart the Badger, looking around, puzzled.

"Those pesky kids, of course!" growled Harry the Badger.

But there was no sign of Stinkbomb and Ketchup-Face.

"Grrr!" growled Harry the Badger in an especially growly way, just to prove he was a bad guy. "After them!"

"But we don't know which way they've gone," Stewart the Badger pointed out.

Rolf the Badger kicked him on the bottom because he wanted to prove he was a bad guy as well. All the other badgers laughed, not because it was particularly funny, but just because they were bad guys too.

Harry the Badger sighed a **BIG** sigh. "We're animals, right?" he said. "So we can track 'em down using our animal senses."

"Right," said Stewart the Badger eagerly. "So . . . we should try **touching** them until we find them!"

Rolf the Badger gave him a hard stare. "How're you going to **touch** them before you've found them?"

Stewart the Badger scratched his head. "I see what you mean," he said. "So . . . we should try **tasting** them until we find them?"

Harry the Badger thwacked him on the ear. "We've got five senses, Stewart the Badger," he said. "Figures you'd pick the wrong two for tracking."

"Oh," said Stewart the Badger. "Right. Well . . ." He **looked** all around the clearing, but he couldn't **see** either Stinkbomb or Ketchup-Face, for the very simple reason that they weren't there. Then he tried **smelling** them, but he couldn't smell anything except for the perfumed blossom of the woodland trees, the sweet smell of the woodland flowers, and the **stinky stink** of the woodland trash that had spilled out when they knocked the garbage can over.

So then he **listened** very, very hard, and so did all the other badgers. And after a while, they **heard** something. In fact, they **heard** two somethings.

"Listen!" said Rolf the Badger. "Is it me, or does one of those noises sound like a frightened chicken?"

"Yeah," agreed Harry the Badger, "and the other one sounds like a squirrel with a bow tie playing 'The Wheels on the Bus.'"

"After them!" cried all the other badgers except Stewart the Badger.

"But it sounds like they're miles away," Stewart the Badger pointed out. "We'll never catch them now."

"Oh, yes, we will," said Harry the Badger. "Because you, Stewart the Badger, have failed to notice one very important thing."

"What's that?" asked Stewart the Badger.

"They've left their sports car behind!" said Harry the Badger. "Come on!"

And all the badgers jumped into the sports car and roared out of the clearing, driving much too fast and knocking the garbage can over again as they left.

CHAPTER 11

—— • ——

IN WHICH
THERE IS AN EXCITING CHASE
AND KETCHUP-FACE CLEARS HER THROAT

Then there was a chase, which was really exciting. Stinkbomb and Ketchup-Face ran as quickly as they could, and the badgers drove too fast and caught up with them, and Stinkbomb and Ketchup-Face tried running even faster, but they couldn't, and the chicken got really really frightened and stuck its head out of Stinkbomb's pocket and went **Buk-AWWWWWK!** and then the badgers caught them. Except for the chicken, which jumped out of Stinkbomb's pocket and ran away.

All right, so it doesn't look quite so exciting written down. But it was.

Anyway, then the badgers picked Stinkbomb and Ketchup-Face up and put them in the car.

"HeLP!"

"HELP!" shouted Stinkbomb and Ketchup-Face. But there was no answer. Then they shouted, **"HeMMMMPH! MMMMPH!"** because the badgers had thrown them into the backseat of the car and sat on their faces.

Then the badgers drove back to the clearing where they lived, and carried Stinkbomb and Ketchup-Face into the crumbling apartment building next to their home. There, in a little basement room with horrid brown and mustard-yellow swirly carpet on the walls and orange wallpaper on the floor, the children learned the dreadful fate that was to be theirs.

"Right," said Harry the Badger. "We can't have you two goin' around telling everyone about our **evil** and **wicked** doings."

"No," said Stewart the Badger. "Especially the one where we're going to get rid of King Toothbrush Weasel and replace him with King Harry the Badger."

"Oh," said Ketchup-Face. "We didn't know about that one."

"Didn't you?" said Stewart the Badger, surprised. "What about the one where we're going to take all the moms in Great Kerfuffle prisoner and force them to make us lunches every day?"

"Yeah," agreed Rolf the Badger, "with **worm sandwiches** and **garbage can gravy**!"

"Mmmm! Yum!" said all the other badgers.

"Nope," said Stinkbomb. "We didn't know about that one either."

"What about," said Stewart the Badger, "the one where we're going to put saddles on all the dads and make them give us piggyback rides everywhere?"

Stinkbomb and Ketchup-Face shook their heads.

"Oh," said Stewart the Badger. "Maybe we should let them go. It doesn't look like they *do* know about our evil and wicked doings after all."

Harry the Badger thwacked him on the ear again. "Except that you've just told them, haven't you? So now we've got no choice. Rolf the Badger: fetch . . . **THE BOX!**"

Rolf the Badger fetched a box. It was a big cardboard box.

"Right," said Harry the Badger. "Now for another **evil** and **wicked** doing." He laughed a wicked laugh, and then passed around a box marked **EVIL MUSTACHES**, and each badger took one and twirled it evilly.

"What we're going to do," Harry the Badger went on, "is put you in this box, and then we're going to mail you to the remote mountain kingdom of Bajerstan, where you'll be put to work painting **stripes** on secondhand tigers."

Stinkbomb thought about this. The idea of being put in a cardboard box and mailed to the remote mountain kingdom of Bajerstan and then being put to work painting **stripes** on second-hand tigers certainly sounded interesting, but he wasn't sure he would actually like it.

Ketchup-Face, on the other hand, was extremely indignant. "You can't put me in a box and mail me to the remote mountain kingdom of Bajerstan and make me paint **stripes** on secondhand tigers!" she protested. "What about my fans?"

"What fans?" demanded Rolf the Badger.

Ketchup-Face straightened in a most digni-fied manner. "When I'm grown up," she said, "I'm going to be a famous singer, and people will come for miles around to see me, and if I'm not there because I'm painting **stripes** on secondhand tigers in the remote mountain kingdom of Bajer-stan, they're going to be all disappointed."

"Oh," said Harry the Badger. "That's a shame. Oh, well, never mind."

"Never mind?" said Ketchup-Face. *"Never mind?"*

"Um . . . maybe she could sing a song for us now," suggested Stewart the Badger, who liked songs and was aware that we hadn't had one since Chapter Two.

"Good idea, Stewart the Badger!" exclaimed Harry the Badger.

"Is it?" asked Stewart the Badger in surprise. He wasn't used to having good ideas.

"Not really," admitted Harry the Badger. "It's

probably a stupid idea, but let's do it anyway. All right, little girl: what are you going to sing for us?"

Ketchup-Face cleared her throat. "I'm going to sing a song which is a work of complete genius," she said. "It's probably the best song in the world, and it's called 'Blueberry Jam.'"

CHAPTER 12

IN WHICH
KETCHUP-FACE SINGS

Blueberry jam," sang Ketchup-Face.

"BLueBeRRy Jam

BLueBeRRy Jam, blueberry jam

BLueBeRRy, blueberry, blueberry Jam

BLuey, bLuey, bLuey

BLuey, bLuey, bLuey, bLuey

BLuey, bLuey, bLueBeRRy Jam

BLueBeRRy Jam

BLueBeRRy Jam

BLueBeRRy

BLueBeRRy

BLueBeRRy

BLueBeRRy

Jaaaaaaaam!!!!!"

The badgers applauded politely.

"Well done," said Harry the Badger. "Right—into the box you go."

Ketchup-Face fixed him with a steely glare. "I haven't finished yet," she said. "That was just the first verse."

"Oh—sorry," said Harry the Badger. "I thought there only was one."

"I wrote some more," said Ketchup-Face, with a touch of pride. "Because the first verse was so good, only it needed more jam."

And she cleared her throat once more, and began to sing the second verse.

CHAPTER 13

—·—

IN WHICH
KETCHUP-FACE SINGS
THE SECOND VERSE

Raspberry jam," sang Ketchup-Face.

"RASPBERRY JAM
RASPBERRY JAM, RASPBERRY JAM
RASPBERRY, RASPBERRY, RASPBERRY JAM
RASPY, RASPY, RASPY
RASPY, RASPY, RASPY, RASPY
RASPBERRY JAM
RASPBERRY JAM
RASPBERRY
JAaaaaaaaaAM!!!!!"

The badgers were about to put their paws together when Ketchup-Face fixed them with another steely glare.

"There's more?" inquired Harry the Badger hesitantly.

Ketchup-Face nodded, and began to sing the next verse.

CHAPTER 14

—— • ——

IN WHICH
KETCHUP-FACE SINGS
THE THIRD VERSE

The third verse was about gooseberry jam.

This time, Ketchup-Face got the steely glare in before the badgers had time to applaud.

Then she continued.

CHAPTER 15

IN WHICH
KETCHUP-FACE SINGS THE TWENTY-SEVENTH VERSE

The twenty-seventh verse was about redcurrant jam.

CHAPTER 16

IN WHICH
KETCHUP-FACE SINGS
THE FIFTY-THIRD VERSE

The fifty-third verse was about cauliflower jam.

CHAPTER 17

—·—

IN WHICH
KETCHUP-FACE SINGS
THE SEVEN HUNDRED AND
EIGHTIETH VERSE

E lephant jam," sang Ketchup-Face.

"ELePHant Jam

ELePHant Jam, eLePHant Jam

ELePHant, eLePHant, eLePHant Jam

eLLy, eLLy, eLLy, eLLy

ELLy, eLLy, eLePHant Jam

ELePHant Jam

ELePHant Jam

ELePHant

Jaaaaaaaaaam!!!!!"

Stewart the Badger yawned, and Ketchup-Face fixed him with another steely glare. This was the five hundred and third steely glare she'd fixed a badger with since the song began, and she felt she was getting rather good at it.

"Did you say something?" she asked coldly.

"Um, no, not at all," Stewart the Badger said miserably. Somewhere around the two hundred and fiftieth verse—the one beginning "Daffodil jam"—the other badgers had sneaked off, leaving him in charge with strict instructions to call them when Ketchup-Face had finished her song. Unfortunately, this didn't seem to be about to happen.

CHAPTER 18

— · —

IN WHICH
KETCHUP-FACE SINGS
THE FOUR THOUSAND
SEVEN HUNDRED AND
SIXTY-NINTH VERSE

Micropachycephalosaurus jam," sang Ketchup-Face.

"Micropachycephalosaurus jam
Micropachycephalosaurus jam,
Micropachycephalosaurus jam
Micropachycephalosaurus,
Micropachycephalosaurus,
Micro, micro, micro,
Micro, micro, micro
Micropachycephalosaurus
jam

MicropachycePHALOSauRuS Jam
MicroPachycePHALOSauRuS Jam
MicroPachycePHALOSauRuS
MicRoPACHYCePHALOSauRuS
Jaaaaaaaaam!!!

MICRO
PACHY
CEPHALO
SAURUS
JAM

90

She fixed Stewart the Badger with another steely glare as he got up.

"I HaveN't fiNiSHeD yet!"

she said. "And all the other badgers have sneaked off. You have to stay and be my audience."

"Um, feel free to carry on without me," said Stewart the Badger, wriggling uncomfortably. "I'll be back in a minute. It's just that, um, I need to go for a poo."

And he made a dash for the door.

CHAPTER 19

— • —

IN WHICH
KETCHUP-FACE IS INTERRUPTED

Quick!" said Stinkbomb. "Let's get out of here!"

Ketchup-Face fixed him with a steely glare. "I haven't finished my song!" she said.

"You can finish it later," Stinkbomb told her.

"But I'm almost at the best part!"

"Look," Stinkbomb said, "either you can keep singing—and then, when you finish the song, the badgers will put us in a cardboard box and mail us to the remote mountain kingdom of Bajerstan, where we'll be put to work painting **stripes** on secondhand tigers—or we can escape and go home, and then you can sing the rest of your song to Mom and Dad after the end of the story."

Ketchup-Face thought about this. "Mom and Dad would probably like my song, wouldn't they?" she said.

Stinkbomb nodded. "I bet they'd love it."

"What about the secondhand tigers?" Ketchup-Face asked. "They'd like it too, wouldn't they?"

Stinkbomb shook his head. "Probably not," he said.

"Oh," said Ketchup-Face. "Are you sure?"

"Pretty sure," Stinkbomb said. **"Tigers have awful taste in music."**

"Oh, okay," Ketchup-Face said. "I wouldn't want the tigers to be disappointed, that's all. Time to escape, then!"

And they escaped.

Or, at least, they did the first bit of escaping, which involved tiptoeing to the elevator. It was broken, but Ketchup-Face fixed it with a steely

glare, and they got in and went up to the ground floor and tiptoed out the front door. Unfortunately, as soon as they had done that, they found themselves entirely surrounded by badgers.

"Hey!" said Harry the Badger gruffly. "What're you doing escaping, when you should be finishing your song and getting into a box?"

"Yeah!" agreed Rolf the Badger. "And what've you done with Stewart the Badger?"

"I'll be down in a minute," came a high squeaky voice from an upstairs window. "I'm just wiping my bottom."

The badgers growled. They were in a very bad mood by this point. Not only had most of them not had anything to say yet; it looked as if most of them weren't even going to be given a **name** before the end of the story. They closed in on our heroes, and it looked as if this time there was no way out. But then . . .

"What's that squeaking noise?" said Ketchup-Face.

The badgers turned and saw a horrifying sight, except that it wasn't very horrifying. But it was definitely a sight, and they saw it. Coming toward them—most of the time, except when it veered off to one side—was the little shopping cart, and

sitting proudly upright in the little shopping cart
was King Toothbrush Weasel, and sitting on King
Toothbrush Weasel's head, nesting in the center
of his crown, was the frightened chicken.
"I say!" said King Toothbrush Weasel
as the little shopping cart
drew near and steered
sideways into a tree.

"What are you two doing here in the middle of all these antelopes?"

"They're not antelopes, they're badgers," said Stinkbomb, opening *How to Identify a Badger* to a picture of a badger and handing it to King Toothbrush Weasel.

"Oh, yes," said King Toothbrush Weasel, looking at the picture. "So they are. The octopus told me you were in trouble, so we've come to help."

"What octopus?" said Ketchup-Face.

"This one, of course," said King Toothbrush Weasel, pointing at the frightened chicken. "Well—it didn't exactly tell me, but it did a mime and drew a picture."

"And I heard your cries for help," said the little shopping cart, "and my mom said my room was almost clean and I'd worked very hard and I could finish it later, so I came too. And luckily someone's been driving a sports car too fast in the enchanted wood, and they've **squashed** all the brambles and bracken down, so I can get in now."

"Buk-AWWWWWK!" added the frightened chicken.

The badgers started muttering darkly, because many of them felt it wasn't fair that even a frightened chicken should get to say more than them.

"Here I am," said Stewart the Badger, bursting through the doors behind Stinkbomb and Ketchup-Face. "Have I missed anything?"

Rolf the Badger looked at him suspiciously. "Did you wash your paws?" he asked.

Stewart the Badger blushed. "Whoops!" he said, and disappeared again.

"So now," continued King Toothbrush Weasel, "I shall rescue you from these **wicked . . .**" —here he paused and checked the book again— "badgers."

"Oh, yeah?" said Harry the Badger. "You and whose army?"

"Me and *my* army, of course!" said King Toothbrush Weasel.

"Meow," said the army, emerging from

behind him and springing gracefully up onto the edge of the basket.

"Ooooooh," murmured the badgers nervously. They'd never seen a whole army before.

"Right!" said Malcolm the Cat. **"You're all under arrest."**

"Are we really?" asked Rolf the Badger.

"No, not really," said Malcolm the Cat. "You can all go, as long as you promise not to do it again. Okay?"

The badgers nodded and began to shuffle away.

"Oh, hold on a minute," Malcolm the Cat said. "My mistake. You *are* under arrest after all."

"Awww," said the badgers, and they all came and stood in front of Malcolm the Cat and waited to be handcuffed.

"Although," said Malcolm the Cat, "I suppose if you were very good, I could let you go . . ."

And then, as the badgers began to shuffle hopefully away again, he added, "Or maybe not."

The doors to the apartment building opened

again, and Stewart the Badger emerged once more. "Have I missed anything?" he asked.

"Yeah," said Harry the Badger glumly. "We're all being arrested by the army."

Stewart the Badger looked at the army. "But it's only a cat," he said.

"Oh, yeah," said all the badgers. "So it is."

And they grabbed Stinkbomb and Ketchup-Face and King Toothbrush Weasel and Malcolm the Cat and the little shopping cart and the frightened chicken, and put them in the cardboard box, and mailed them to the remote mountain kingdom of Bajerstan.

CHAPTER 20

———— • ————

IN WHICH
OUR HEROES GET BORED
IN A CARDBOARD BOX

It was very cramped in the box. Stinkbomb
ended up with King Toothbrush Weasel's elbow
up his nose and Malcolm the Cat's tail in his ear,
and the frightened chicken laid an egg on his head.

"Hey!" said Ketchup-Face from her folded-up
position underneath the little shopping cart. "I
can get my toes in my mouth!"

Stinkbomb tried this, and found that he could
get his toes in his mouth as well, which was
at least something to do to pass the time. They

discovered that they could get their toes in each other's mouths too, but King Toothbrush Weasel wouldn't let them try to get their toes in his mouth because he said that sort of thing wasn't very royal.

When that got boring, they played **I Spy,** which wasn't much fun because the badgers had taken Stinkbomb's flashlight, so everyone's turn began, "I spy with my little eye something beginning with **D**," and then everyone else guessed Darkness and was right every time—except when it was Ketchup-Face's turn. Her **D** turned out to be for **D**oris, who she said was her imaginary friend. This made Stinkbomb a bit annoyed because he knew Ketchup-Face's imaginary friend was named Salary, which didn't begin with **D** even the way Ketchup-Face spelled it.

"Anyway," he complained, "how can you see her in the dark?"

"Because she's imaginary," Ketchup-Face explained.

Fairly soon they stopped playing that, and Stinkbomb and Ketchup-Face took turns asking "Are we there yet?" every five minutes.

And all the time, the box was **bumping** and **jolting** and doing all those things that boxes do when they're in the mail.

At last, they felt the box being set down, and there was the unmistakable sound of a door being knocked on.

"Is this the secondhand tiger factory?" asked Ketchup-Face. "I can't hear any tigers."

A moment later, the unmistakable sound of a door being knocked on came again. Then there was the unmistakable sound of a mailman filling out one of those "Sorry we missed you" cards and dropping it into a mail slot, and then the unmistakable feeling of being carried around to be left behind a garbage can at the back of the house. And then came the unmistakable sound of a mailman driving away, followed by the unmistakable sound of nothing happening.

After a little while, Ketchup-Face said, "I'm bored of being in this box. Can we get out now?"

"I'm afraid we're still trapped in here," King Toothbrush Weasel told her. "If someone doesn't come and let us out, we could be stuck in this box until it rains enough to make the cardboard all soggy and mushy."

Stinkbomb thought about this. The idea of being stuck in a box until it rained enough to make the cardboard **soggy** and **mushy** certainly sounded interesting, but he wasn't sure he would actually like it.

"If only we had a knife," said the little shopping cart, vainly bashing its basket against the side of the box in a futile attempt to escape.

"But I do!" said Stinkbomb in great excitement, suddenly remembering. Wriggling his hand around, he managed to reach into his pocket— and after pulling out a **comic book,**

a bag of chips,

a cardboard elephant,
a telephone pole,
an interestingly shaped rock,
and a squirrel,

he eventually produced a shiny and very sharp **pocketknife**, with which he cut a door in the wall of the box.

CHAPTER 21

IN WHICH
OUR HEROES ESCAPE FROM THE CARDBOARD BOX AND KETCHUP-FACE MAKES A DISCOVERY

We're free!" shouted the little shopping cart.

"Hurrah!" yelled King Toothbrush Weasel.

"Buk-AWWWWWK!" said the frightened chicken.

Malcolm the Cat had gone to sleep in the little shopping cart's basket during the game of **I Spy**, so he didn't say anything, and neither did Stinkbomb, who just looked pleased with himself. But Ketchup-Face was eyeing the pocketknife **suspiciously**.

"Is that new?" she asked.

Stinkbomb nodded. "I bought it yesterday," he said. "I've been wanting one for ages."

"Where did you get the money for it?" Ketchup-Face said.

Stinkbomb rolled his eyes impatiently. "If you *need* to know," he said, "I had twenty dollars in my piggy bank, and I . . ."

And then he stopped.

"Oh," he said. He went red.

"Oh," he said again.

And then he said, "OW!" because Ketchup-Face was jumping UP and down on his toes.

"you idiot, Stinkbomb!" she was yelling.

"you useless pile of DANDRUFF,

You ENORMOUS cabbagey cushion!

You STUPID frog-flavored envelope!”

She paused to take a breath. "We've been scared in a dark wood and chased by badgers and put in a box and mailed to the remote mountain kingdom of Bajerstan to paint **stripes** on secondhand tigers for the **rest of our lives**, and I didn't even get to finish my song, and now it turns out the badgers didn't even steal your money at all, not even a little bit! It's all your fault!"

King Toothbrush Weasel was suddenly looking very serious. "You mean the badgers aren't **evil** and **wicked** after all?" he said. "Oh, dear. Poor innocent creatures. We have misjudged them."

"Well, not—**OW**—really," explained Stinkbomb. "I mean, they did—**OW**—put us in a box and mail us to the—OW—remote mountain kingdom of Bajer—**OW**—stan."

"Yes," added Ketchup-Face breathlessly, still jumping. "And they're going to force all the mommies to make their awful lunches, and make all the daddies give them piggyback rides."

"That's right," said Stinkbomb. "And—ow—they're going to replace you with—OW—King Harry the Badger. Ow."

"Ow," agreed Ketchup-Face as she fell over, exhausted, to lie panting on the grass.

"What?" said King Toothbrush Weasel, horror-struck. "Overthrow me and put a badger on the throne of Great Kerfuffle? But . . . but that's tree-house!"

"Um, I think you mean *treason*, Your Majesty," said the little shopping cart shyly.

"Nonsense!" said King Toothbrush Weasel. "A treason is a little house in the branches of a tree. Anyway, we have to stop them!"

"But how?" asked Ketchup-Face. "We're in the remote mountain kingdom of Bajerstan."

"Er, no we're not," said the little shopping cart. They looked around, and found it was true.

"Well, bless my soul," said King Toothbrush Weasel. "How did we get here?"

It was like a miracle, or at least like one of those times when the mailman delivers a package to the wrong house. Far from being in the remote mountain kingdom of Bajerstan, they were behind a garbage can in back of Stinkbomb and Ketchup-Face's very own home, on a hillside above the tiny village of Loose Pebbles.

The little shopping cart was examining the box. "Look!" it said. "Someone's changed the address!"

Stinkbomb looked. "Oh, yeah," he said. "I forgot I'd done that."

"*You* did this?" asked King Toothbrush Weasel.

Stinkbomb nodded. "Yeah," he said. "While Ketchup-Face was singing her song. During the verse about duck-billed platypus jam. I got a little bored, so I got out a pen and wrote my name and address on the box."

"And a good thing too!" said King Toothbrush Weasel. "But how will we stop the badgers from doing any more **evil** and **wicked** doings?"

They all went **"Hmm,"** and scratched their heads.

Then Stinkbomb jumped up and pointed at the garbage can. "That garbage can has given me an idea!" he said. "But we'll have to be really quick!"

"Why?" asked King Toothbrush Weasel worriedly.

"Because we're almost at the end of the story," explained Ketchup-Face.

"And we need to get to a shop," added Stink-bomb.

"Quickly, Starlight, my noble steed!"

shouted Ketchup-Face.

"Who?" said the little shopping cart. "Oh—oh, right."

"Ow!" said Malcolm the Cat, waking up, as Ketchup-Face jumped into the basket of the cart and sat on him. **"Ow! Ow!"** he added as Stink-bomb and King Toothbrush Weasel and the frightened chicken scrambled in after her.

"Where to?" asked the little shopping cart eagerly.

"Full speed ahead!" yelled Stinkbomb.

"To the village of Loose Pebbles!"

CHAPTER 22

IN WHICH
THE BADGERS GET WHAT'S COMING TO THEM
AND ALL ENDS HAPPILY

As soon as the sun had set, the badgers crept out of the enchanted wood and stole across the valley. A-snuffling and a-scurrying they went, their teeth and claws all gleaming and badgery in the moonlight. Their hearts were filled with **evil** and **wickedness**, and their minds were filled with thoughts of treason, and their tummies were filled with worms and bits of garbage.

The other creatures sensed with their animal senses that the badgers were on the move, and they were filled with fear. The cows cowered, and the quails quailed, and the foxes lay in bed recovering from having been **squashed** by the pigs. Some of the braver animals made their feelings clear as the badgers passed by—a snake **hissed**; a snail **booed**; a blackbird blew a **raspberry**; a raspbird blew a **blackberry**; a hedgehog wrote an **angry letter** to the newspapers—but mostly they just hid, knowing that whatever the badgers were up to, they were up to no good.

But as the badgers, intent on **evil**, came over the hill and entered the valley that led down to the tiny village of Loose Pebbles, they saw a marvelous sight such as they had never seen before.

It was a trail of garbage cans, all of them **shiny** and **new**, leading right through the village and just begging to be **knocked over**.

"Yes!" shouted the badgers. And they were just about to rush forward and knock all the garbage cans over when Harry the Badger spoke.

"Hold on!" he said, in a voice so commanding that the badgers all immediately held on. "We can't go knocking all these garbage cans over!"

"But . . . but we're badgers!" said Stewart the Badger.

"Yeah!" agreed Rolf the Badger. "What kind of badgers would we be if we went about **not** knocking garbage cans over?"

Harry the Badger folded his paws and looked sternly at them. "Quiet badgers, that's what kind," he said. "We're supposed to be quiet so we can get to the palace under cover of darkness and make **me** king!"

"Yeah," said Rolf the Badger, "but we could just knock over a few garbage cans on the way, couldn't we?"

"Plee-ease!" added Stewart the Badger, and all the other badgers put their paws together, stuck their bottom lips out, and made their eyes really really big, because they'd once heard from a little girl that it's a good way to get what you want.

"No!" said Harry the Badger sternly.

"Awwwwww!" said all the badgers.

"Well," said Harry the Badger, "maybe just one. As long as you're very, very quiet."

"Hurray!" whispered all the badgers, and they set off again. They were as silent as they could be, although Stewart the Badger kept whistling under his breath because the tune to "Blueberry

Jam" was stuck in his head. It wasn't a particularly catchy tune, but he had heard it four thousand seven hundred and sixty-nine times.

Rolf the Badger had to keep nudging him to be quiet.

Into the village the badgers tiptoed, agog with wonder at the number and variety of garbage cans on display. Which one should they knock over? The **square** green one by the rug store? The **cylindrical** bronze one by the drug store? The tall red **bottle-shaped** one by the hug store? Each was so tempting—but how to choose?

Then, suddenly, they saw it. Their eyes widened with delight and expectation, because each of them knew that if they could knock over only one garbage can, it would have to be this one. It stood at the very end of the street, as tall as a house and twice as wide, gleaming silver in the moonlight. As they stared, the delirious badgers could imagine it crashing to the ground in a more **crashy** and **bangy** way than any garbage can they had ever knocked over.

They looked at one another and exchanged excited nods, and then they **charged!**

In one gigantic mob they ran, hurling themselves toward this **garbage can of all** garbage cans, their hearts filled with **ecstasy** and **rapture** at the naughtiness of what they were about to do. Faster and faster

they raced, until they could not have
stopped if they wanted to—and just
before that moment of sheer joy
when they collided with it
and knocked it **tumbling**
and **clattering**
to the ground . . .

"Pull!" shouted Stinkbomb and Ketchup-Face together, and the two of them with King Toothbrush Weasel and the frightened chicken and all the villagers pulled as hard as they could on the cleverly disguised night-colored rope, which was tied to the enormous garbage can. And the little shopping cart, in its cunning hiding place under the can, heaved and squeaked with all its might, and the can rolled right out of the way.

"Aaaaargh!" yelled the shocked badgers as, unable to stop, they ran headlong into the village jail, which had been hidden behind the garbage can all the time.

"Oh, no!" they added as Malcolm the Cat leapt up and slammed the door behind them.

"Caught you, you horrid old badgers!" Ketchup-Face said happily. "And now you have to be in jail forever and ever!"

"Well, not forever and ever," said Stinkbomb. "Just until the end of your sentence."

"That doesn't seem very long," said Ketchup-Face. "Just till the end of a sentence? It should be till the end of the whole story, at least. Except that's not very long now."

"Actually," said King Toothbrush Weasel, "the penalty for treehouse is to stay in jail until half-way through the story after next."

"That seems fair," said the little shopping cart. **"Buk-AWWWWK!"** said the frightened chicken.

"Wait a minute," said Malcolm the Cat. "These don't look like the same badgers to me. Maybe we should let them go." He opened the jail door. Then he said, "Or maybe they are the same badgers," and shut it. "On the other hand . . ."

"Grrr!" growled Rolf the Badger. "Just you wait!"

"Yeah!" agreed Harry the Badger. "We'll get out of here, and then we'll knock over all the garbage cans in town and do some other **evil** things we haven't thought of yet!"

"Yeah!" chorused all the other badgers, except Stewart the Badger, who had found the jail's games cupboard.

"Hey!" he said. "Anyone want to play Monopoly?"

"Dibs on the little car!" said all the other badgers at once.

"Come on, everyone!" said King Toothbrush Weasel. "Time to celebrate! Let's go to the Loose Pebbles Café!"

"HOORAY!"

said Stinkbomb and Ketchup-Face and the little shopping cart and all the villagers.

"Buk-AWWWWK!" said the frightened chicken.

"Grrrrr!" said the badgers, and they began to drive the little car too fast around the Monopoly board, knocking over the houses and hotels as they went.

A few minutes later, Stinkbomb and Ketchup-Face found themselves in the Loose Pebbles Café, surrounded by admiring villagers and being bought all manner of **delicious treats**. As they told everyone the story of their adventures, King Toothbrush Weasel pinned medals on them. In the café, everything was **warm** and **COZY** and **friendly**, and in the distance they could hear the happy sound of the jail door opening and closing repeatedly.

Only one more thing, they thought, was needed to make the scene completely perfect.

And then, to their delight, they saw two familiar shapes silhouetted on the frosted glass of the café door, and the door began to open.

"Mom! Dad!" cried Stinkbomb.

"Hello, my darlings!" came their mother's voice from outside. "Can we come in? Has the story finished yet?"

"Yes," said Ketchup-Face happily.

"WOULD you LiKE to HEAR MY NEW SONG?"

Blueberry Jam
by Ketchup-Face

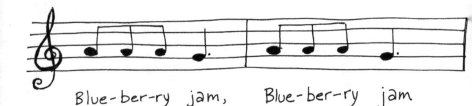

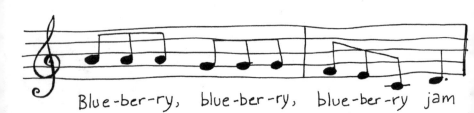

ACKNOWLEDGMENTS

With thanks to everyone who's ever done, said, or been anything that has ended up being stolen by me and put into this book. Particular thanks go to: Toby Perot for inspiring Ketchup-Face's song; Saskia Honey Jarlett McAndrews for her exceptional king-naming skills; my old and dear friend John Sandford, wondering if you'll remember which bit I stole from you; and Malcolm the cat for being a cat named Malcolm. Also to Rob Kempner for transcribing the music for "Blueberry Jam."

And particular particular thanks go to Noah and Cara for all the inspiration and ideas, help and encouragement, and for lighting up my life even when the curtains are drawn and I'm trying to sleep. Without you, there'd be no Great Kerfuffle.

—J.D.

Jo Cotterill

JOHN DOUGHERTY was born in Larne, Northern Ireland, and not many years later they made him go to school—an experience he didn't find entirely enjoyable. Fortunately, the joys of reading helped him through the difficult times. It's therefore not completely surprising that when he grew up he became first a teacher (the nice sort), and then a writer of stories and poetry to make children giggle. He also writes songs, some of which he performs with First Draft, a band made up of three children's authors and a bookseller. He now lives in England with his two wonderful children, the original Stinkbomb and Ketchup-Face.

COMING SOON

QUEST FOR THE
MAGIC PORCUPINE